EXPLORING DINOSAURS

TRICERATOPS

By Susan H. Gray

THE CHILD'S WORLD®
CHANHASSEN, MINNESOTA

The Child's World

Published in the United States of America by The Child's World®
P.O. Box 326, Chanhassen, MN 55317-0326
800-599-READ
www.childsworld.com

Content Adviser:
Peter Makovicky,
Ph.D., Curator,
Field Museum,
Chicago, Illinois

Photo Credits: Ben Klaffke: 10; Kevin Schafer/Corbis: 4; Jonathan Blair/Corbis: 5; Jim Zuckerman/Corbis: 6; Michael S. Yamashita/Corbis: 9; David Muench/Corbis: 14; AFP/Corbis: 15; Reuters NewMedia, Inc./Corbis: 16; Lee Snider/Corbis: 17; Annie Griffiths Belt/Corbis: 20; Douglas Peebles/Corbis: 24; Sanford Agliolo/Corbis: 26–27; Tom McHugh/Photo Researchers, Inc.: 8; Francois Gohier/Photo Researchers, Inc.: 12, 13 (Specimen from Zuni Basin Paleontological Project, Courtesy D. Wolfe, Mesa Southwest Museum, and Gaston Design); Richard T. Nowitz/Photo Researchers, Inc.: 21; Chris Butler/Science Photo Library/Photo Researchers, Inc.: 23; Courtesy of the Smithsonian Institution: 18 (#MNH-30687-C), 19 (#SI 98-27591); A.J. Copley/Visuals Unlimited, Inc.: 11.

The Child's World®: Mary Berendes, Publishing Director

Editorial Directions, Inc.: E. Russell Primm, Editorial Director; Dana Meachen Rau, Line Editor; Katie Marsico, Assistant Editor; Matthew Messbarger, Editorial Assistant; Susan Hindman, Copy Editor; Susan Ashley, Proofreader; Tim Griffin, Indexer; Kerry Reid, Fact Checker; Dawn Friedman, Photo Researcher; Linda S. Koutris, Photo Selector

Original cover art by Todd Marshall

The Design Lab: Kathleen Petelinsek, Design and Page Production

Library of Congress Cataloging-in-Publication Data
Gray, Susan Heinrichs.
 Triceratops / by Susan H. Gray.
   p. cm. — (Exploring dinosaurs)
Includes index.
Summary: Describes what is known about the physical characteristics, behavior, habitat, and life cycle of this horned, plant-eating dinosaur.
 ISBN 1-59296-045-6 (lib. bdg. : alk. paper)
 1. Triceratops—Juvenile literature. [1. Triceratops. 2. Dinosaurs.] I. Title. II. Series.
QE862.O65G7462 2004
567.915'8—dc22   2003018632

TABLE OF CONTENTS

CHAPTER ONE

CATCHING A NAP

The big *Triceratops* (try-SEHR-uh-tops) was sound asleep.

He stood in a patch of ferns, breathing loudly. Every time

he breathed out, the ferns under his nose fluttered. Four smaller

Triceratops bones have been found in western North America, both in Canada and the United States. About 50 Triceratops skulls and some parts of skeletons have been found.

Do these Triceratops *remind you of anyone? How about rhinos? Like* Triceratops, *a rhinoceros has horns on its face that it uses to protect itself from sudden harm. If a* Triceratops *was threatened, it probably charged at its enemy just like a rhinoceros does.*

Triceratops were feeding on ferns nearby. One of them nudged her

baby, pushing him to exercise his little legs.

Suddenly in the distance, a *Tyrannosaurus rex* (tie-RAN-uh-

SORE-uhss REX), also called *T. rex,* appeared. The herd of

Triceratops *had to be on the lookout for* T. rex, *otherwise, it would be lunch for the* T. rex. *Recently, fossils of droppings from a* T. rex *were found in Canada. These* T. rex *droppings were 65 million years old and contained bones from a plant-eating dinosaur, most likely a* Triceratops.

Triceratops looked up. It quickly moved into position, forming a line facing the *T. rex*. The mother shoved her baby behind the group. The dinosaurs began stamping their feet. They bobbed their huge heads up and down. The racket woke the sleeping dinosaur. He blinked his eyes and shook himself awake. Then he moved into line with the others.

Still far off, the *T. rex* stopped in her tracks. She stood frozen for a few seconds, watching the fierce display. Then she turned and slowly walked away. One by one, the members of the herd stopped their stamping. They stood in silence, watching the *T. rex* disappear in the distance. Once out of danger, they returned to their feeding. Still sleepy, the big *Triceratops* blinked a few times, then lowered his eyelids. He dropped his head and nodded off again.

CHAPTER TWO

WHAT IS A *TRICERATOPS*?

The *Triceratops* is a dinosaur that lived from about 70 to 65 million years ago. Its name is taken from Greek words that mean "three-horned face." This name refers to the three large horns on the dinosaur's head.

From snout to tail, the **reptile** was 25 to 30 feet (7.6 to 9.1

Scientists cannot decide how many species, or kinds, of Triceratops *have been found. Some believe there is only one species,* Triceratops horridus. *Others believe that there are two or more species.*

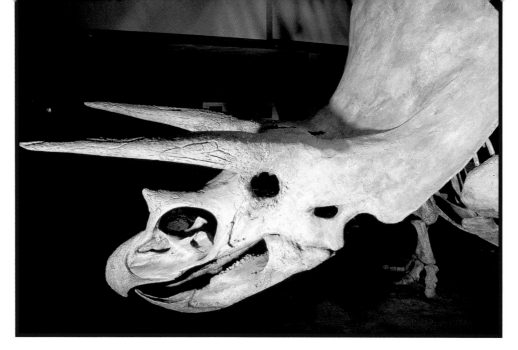

Some say that you can tell Triceratops *was a plant eater from its beak. This beak would have been very useful for clipping branches. Also, the flat, grinding teeth would have been good for chewing plant material.*

meters) long. It stood on four massive legs, the back ones longer than the front. The dinosaur was about 10 feet (3 m) tall at the highest point on its back. It may have weighed up to 6 tons or more. *Triceratops* walked on its toes, probably holding its short, thick tail in the air.

The dinosaur's head was enormous—nearly 10 feet (3 m) long. Its snout ended in a hard beak. A short horn above the beak pointed forward and up. Two larger horns stuck out above its eyes. A huge, bony collar, called a frill, spread out from the back of its head.

Triceratops probably traveled in groups. To defend itself, it may have charged at its enemies. Or the group might have gathered in a line or circle, all of the dinosaurs facing outward and stamping their feet. That would have been enough to scare away most attackers.

Even if a **predator** did attack, *Triceratops* would be ready. A well-aimed thrust with one of those horns could strike an enemy dead.

Triceratops *probably lived in an environment with a very large food supply. We can assume this based on the enormous size of the dinosaur.*

WHAT A BONEHEAD!

The bony head of the *Triceratops* was very large. It was about one-third the length of the dinosaur's whole body. Scientists believe the dinosaur's head alone weighed between 400 and 600 pounds (181 and 272 kilograms). The two massive horns pointing forward just above the eyes were called brow horns. A third, smaller horn called the nasal (NAY-zul) horn was right above the nose. Brow horns that are more than 3 feet (0.9 m) long have been found. Nasal horns grew to about 1 foot (30 centimeters) in length. When the *Triceratops* dinosaur was alive, a covering on the horn made it even longer!

Triceratops had a hollow space in its skull that may have acted as a shock absorber. If the dinosaur rammed its heavy head into something, the space in the skull would cushion the brain. The dinosaur probably rammed its head pretty often—sometimes into attackers and sometimes into others in the herd. The males may have butted each other with their heads. The winners would then get a chance to find a mate.

The bony frill of the *Triceratops* was most impressive. Scientists have suggested several ideas about its purpose. Maybe it protected the dinosaur's neck. It might have been used to scare off enemies. The frill could have fooled an attacker into thinking the *Triceratops* was much bigger than it was. Perhaps the frill helped *Triceratops* attract a mate. Or maybe it helped the dinosaur adjust its temperature. *Triceratops* might have stood in the warm sun or cool breeze. Its frill would have been the first body part to warm up or cool down.

CHAPTER THREE

DID *TRICERATOPS* ACT
LIKE ITS RELATIVES?

*T*riceratops belongs to a group of dinosaurs called the ceratop-

sians (SEHR-uh-TOP-see-unz), meaning "horn-faced."

These dinosaurs had many things in common. Some had frills.

Some had horns on their heads. Some had mouths with beaks.

Because the ceratopsians looked alike, some scientists believe

they may have acted alike. Scientists have found bone beds of

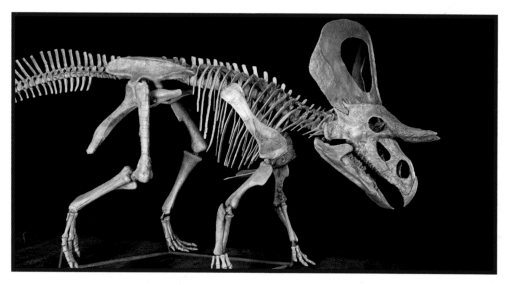

Triceratops *was one of the ceratopsians. The very first ceratopsians lived about 144 million years ago, many years before* Triceratops *was alive.*

At Dinosaur National Monument in Dinosaur, Colorado, you can see one of the best dinosaur bone beds in the world. A total of 11 species of dinosaur have been found there.

ceratopsians. A bone bed is an area that contains many skeletons.

It might be a place where a group of dinosaurs died together. If they

died together as a group, they may have lived together as a group.

Scientists have also found ceratopsian trackways. These are sets

of dinosaur footprints. Trackways show that ceratopsians may have traveled together in a group. They may have kept the babies and younger dinosaurs in the center of the group, where it was safer. Older adults may have kept to the edge and protected the young ones.

Maybe *Triceratops* acted like its ceratopsian relatives. It might have lived in a herd. It might have traveled with a group of young and old together. Right now, though, no one can say for sure.

Tracks and trackways are very important to scientists. Tracks give them valuable clues about where and when certain dinosaurs lived, how they lived, how individual dinosaurs behaved, and how they interacted with other dinosaurs.

CHAPTER FOUR

WHO DISCOVERED TRICERATOPS?

In 1888, John Bell Hatcher was looking for fossils in Wyoming. Fossils are the remains of **ancient** plants and animals. Dinosaur footprints, eggs, and bones are types of fossils. Hatcher worked for Othniel Charles Marsh, a famous paleontologist (PAY-lee-un-TAWL-uh-jist). Paleontologists are people who study fossils and ancient life.

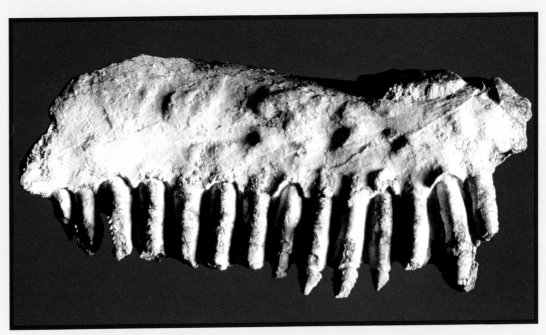

Fossils provide paleontologists with a lot of important information. This is a fossil jawbone from a plant-eating dinosaur that lived about 230 million years ago.

The Smithsonian Institution is the largest museum complex in the world.
The dinosaur exhibits alone include more than 1,500 specimens.

Hatcher found part of a huge skull. It was from a dinosaur that no

one had ever seen before. Marsh, Hatcher's boss, gave it the name

Triceratops.

Over the next few years, Hatcher found parts of more than 40 *Tricer-*

atops skeletons. He sent many of the bones to the Smithsonian Institu-

tion. The Smithsonian is a large museum complex in Washington, D.C.

Scientists at the Smithsonian put together the first *Triceratops*

skeleton. There were some problems, though. They had to use

bones from at least ten different *Triceratops* skeletons. This was

because no one had yet found a complete skeleton. Some of the

bones were not the right size. Someone even put the feet of another

dinosaur on the skeleton! With Hatcher's help, however, the

scientists did the best they could. The skeleton went on display

Norman Boss was a Smithsonian Institution employee who worked to
get the Triceratops *skeleton ready for display in 1905.*

Today, scientists at the Smithsonian are working on a plan to dismantle the original Triceratops *skeleton and make a perfect computer-generated replica to stand in its place. Already they have an accurate "digital dinosaur" which can be sent to researchers as easily as E-mail!*

in 1905. People came from all over to see it.

In 1998, scientists started working to fix some of the problems.

They found bones that were the right size. They gave the skeleton the

proper feet. They even fixed up bones that had started to fall apart.

A nationwide contest was held to name the dinosaur. A 10 year

old boy in Wyoming suggested the name "Hatcher." The museum

liked his idea of naming the dinosaur after its discoverer. Now,

Hatcher, the fixed-up *Triceratops,* proudly stands in the museum.

PICKING THE BONES CLEAN

John Bell Hatcher did some amazing work. Like most paleontologists, he did not find nice, clean bones. He usually
found broken bones embedded in rocks. The rock surround-
ing a bone is called its matrix (MAY-trix). If paleontologists
pry the bone out of its matrix, they will tear up the bone. So
they dig out a bone and leave some of the matrix on. They
send the whole thing to a laboratory. There, people carefully
clean all the matrix off.

People who clean bones and get them ready for muse-
ums are called preparators (pruh-PEHR-uh-turz). They work

slowly and skillfully. They often use tiny instruments. Sometimes they use little hammers and chisels. Sometimes they
use dental picks, just like your dentist uses to clean your
teeth. Sometimes they use tiny electric tools.

One tool sprays a powderlike material on fossils to blast
away the matrix. Another tool works like a little jackham-
mer. Every minute, it makes thousands of tiny beats against
the matrix, until the rock falls away. A little grinder, much
like a dentist's drill, smooths off the last pieces of matrix.
Fixing up fossils takes
lots of time and patience.

John Bell Hatcher
dug up many *Triceratops*
skulls and sent them
off to the preparators.
One of these skulls
with its matrix weighed
more than 6,000 pounds
(2,722 kg). It took a
huge wagon and a team
of horses to haul it
away. Just imagine
what a job it was to
clean that skull!

CHAPTER FIVE

ENVIRONMENT OF THE *TRICERATOPS*

Triceratops lived during a time called the Cretaceous (kreh-TAY-shuss) period. This period started about 144 million years ago and lasted almost 80 million years. *Triceratops* lived for only the last few million years of this period.

The Earth then was quite different from the one we know today. The **continents** were much closer together. Great, two-legged dinosaurs, such as *Tyrannosaurus rex,* roamed North America. Four-legged dinosaurs, such as *Triceratops* and another horn-face called *Torosaurus* (TORE-uh-SORE-uhss), walked the Earth.

T. rex probably **preyed** on *Triceratops*. We know this from looking at *Triceratops* bones. In the 1990s, a paleontologist found

*Just think, dinosaurs of all shapes and sizes once roamed
in the very place where you are standing.*

Cycads have very sharp leaves that surround the central trunk. A Triceratops might have used his beak to tear off these spiky leaves before eating the trunk.

an interesting *Triceratops* hip bone. It had 50 bite marks thought to be made by *T. rex* teeth! *Triceratops* did not prey on other dinosaurs, however. It ate only plant material. Plants of the time included cycads (SY-kadz) and ferns. There were also oak and walnut trees. Grass had not yet appeared.

Some small mammals the size of mice, rats, and opossums skittered about the ground. Large mammals were not around yet. By the time humans appeared, dinosaurs had been **extinct** for millions of years.

CHAPTER SIX

THE GREAT EXTINCTION

For some reason, all dinosaurs became extinct about 65 million years ago. All over the world, they just died out. No one is certain why this happened. Scientists have put forth some ideas. Dinosaurs might have died because the Earth became too hot or too cold. Perhaps it was because many volcanoes erupted and filled the air with ash.

Today, many scientists think a giant **asteroid** slammed into Earth about 65 million years ago. They believe it happened on the Yucatan Peninsula (YOO-kuh-TAN pen-IN-suh-luh) in Mexico. There is a huge **crater** (KRAY-ter) there where something enormous hit the Earth. The crash caused billions of tons of soil and ash to fly up into the air. The sun's light was blotted out. The Earth

*Many scientists today believe that a giant asteroid crashed into Earth about
65 million years ago. It may have been the reason that Triceratops, T. rex,
and all the other dinosaurs disappeared.*

grew dark and cold. Scientists believe that these changes caused most plants and animals, including all of the dinosaurs, to die out.

This asteroid idea could be correct. But we may never know for sure what happened to *Triceratops* or what killed the dinosaurs. We may forever be looking for clues to why these giants disappeared.

Glossary

ancient (AYN-shunt) Something that is ancient is very old; from millions of years ago. Ancient leaf imprints are an example of a fossil.

asteroid (ASS-tuh-roid) An asteroid is a rocky body that is smaller than a planet and orbits the sun. A giant asteroid may have crashed into Earth millions of years ago and caused the dinosaurs to die out.

continents (KON-tih-nents) The great land masses of the Earth are called continents. Long ago, the Earth's continents were in different locations.

crater (KRAY-tur) A crater is a large, bowl-shaped dip in the Earth's surface. Some scientists think that the large crater in the Yucatan Peninsula was caused by an asteroid hitting the Earth.

extinct (ek-STINGKT) Something that is extinct no longer exists. Scientists have several ideas about how the dinosaurs may have become extinct.

predator (PRED-uh-tur) A predator is an animal that hunts and eats other animals. *T. rex* was a predator during the Cretaceous period.

preyed (PRAYD) To prey on something means to hunt it down and eat it. It is likely that *T. rex* preyed upon *Triceratops*.

reptile (REP-tile) A reptile is an air-breathing animal with a backbone and is usually covered with scales or plates. *Triceratops* was a reptile.

Did You Know?

▶ *Triceratops* is the state fossil of South Dakota and the state dinosaur of Wyoming.

▶ For many years, the Smithsonian skeleton of *Triceratops* was getting damaged from the vibrations of people walking by. They were slowly shaking it to pieces.

▶ As preparators clean fossils, they use tiny vacuum cleaners to suck up the dust.

The Geologic Time Scale

TRIASSIC PERIOD

Date: 248 million to 208 million years ago

Fossils: *Coelophysis, Cynodont, Desmatosuchus, Eoraptor, Gerrothorax, Peteinosaurus, Placerias, Plateosaurus, Postosuchus, Procompsognathus, Riojasaurus, Saltopus, Teratosaurus, Thecodontosaurus*

Distinguishing Features: For the most part, the climate in the Triassic period was hot and dry. The first true mammals appeared during this period, as well as turtles, frogs, salamanders, and lizards. Corals could also be found in oceans at this time, although large reefs such as the ones we have today did not yet exist. Evergreen trees made up much of the plant life.

JURASSIC PERIOD

Date: 208 million to 144 million years ago

Fossils: *Allosaurus, Anchisaurus, Apatosaurus, Barosaurus, Brachiosaurus, Ceratosaurus, Compsognathus, Cryptoclidus, Dilophosaurus, Diplodocus, Eustreptospondylus, Hybodus, Janenschia, Kentrosaurus, Liopleurodon, Megalosaurus, Opthalmosaurus, Rhamphorhynchus, Saurolophus, Segisaurus, Seismosaurus, Stegosaurus, Supersaurus, Syntarsus, Ultrasaurus, Vulcanodon, Xiaosaurus*

Distinguishing Features: The climate of the Jurassic period was warm and moist. The first birds appeared during this period. Plant life was also greener and more widespread. Sharks began swimming in Earth's oceans. Although dinosaurs didn't even exist at the beginning of the Triassic period, they ruled Earth by Jurassic times. There was a minor mass extinction toward the end of the Jurassic period.

CRETACEOUS PERIOD

Date: 144 million to 65 million years ago

Fossils: *Acrocanthosaurus, Alamosaurus, Albertosaurus, Anatotitan, Ankylosaurus, Argentinosaurus, Bagaceratops, Baryonyx, Carcharodontosaurus, Carnotaurus, Centrosaurus, Chasmosaurus, Corythosaurus, Didelphodon, Edmontonia, Edmontosaurus, Gallimimus, Gigantosaurus, Hadrosaurus, Hypsilophodon, Iguanodon, Kronosaurus, Lambeosaurus, Leaellynasaura, Maiasaura, Megaraptor, Muttaburrasaurus, Nodosaurus, Ornithocheirus, Oviraptor, Pachycephalosaurus, Panoplosaurus, Parasaurolophus, Pentaceratops, Polacanthus, Protoceratops, Psittacosaurus, Quaesitosaurus, Saltasaurus, Sarcosuchus, Saurolophus, Sauropelta, Saurornithoides, Segnosaurus, Spinosaurus, Stegoceras, Stygimoloch, Styracosaurus, Tapejara, Tarbosaurus, Therizinosaurus, Thescelosaurus, Torosaurus, Trachodon, Triceratops, Troodon, Tyrannosaurus rex, Utahraptor, Velociraptor*

Distinguishing Features: The climate of the Cretaceous period was fairly mild. Flowering plants first appeared in this period, and many modern plants developed. With flowering plants came a greater diversity of insect life. Birds further developed into two types: flying and flightless. A wider variety of mammals also existed. At the end of this period came a great mass extinction that wiped out the dinosaurs, along with several other groups of animals.

How to Learn More

At the Library

Lambert, David, Darren Naish, and Liz Wyse. *Dinosaur Encyclopedia.*
New York: DK Publishing, 2001.

Landau, Elaine. *Triceratops.*
Danbury, Conn.: Children's Press, 1999.

On the Web

Visit our home page for lots of links about *Triceratops:*
http://www.childsworld.com/links.html
Note to Parents, Teachers, and Librarians: We routinely verify our
Web links to make sure they're safe, active sites—so encourage
your readers to check them out!

Places to Visit or Contact

AMERICAN MUSEUM OF NATURAL HISTORY
To view numerous dinosaur fossils, as well
as the fossils of several ancient mammals
Central Park West at 79th Street
New York, NY 10024-5192
212/769-5100

CARNEGIE MUSEUM OF NATURAL HISTORY
To view a variety of dinosaur skeletons, as well as fossils
related to other reptiles, amphibians, and fish that are now extinct
4400 Forbes Avenue
Pittsburgh, PA 15213
412/622-3131

DINOSAUR NATIONAL MONUMENT

To view a huge deposit of dinosaur bones in a natural setting

4545 East Highway 40

Dinosaur, CO 81610-9724

or

DINOSAUR NATIONAL MONUMENT

(QUARRY)

11625 East 1500 South

Jensen, UT 84035

435/781-7700

MUSEUM OF THE ROCKIES

To see real dinosaur fossils, as well as robotic replicas

Montana State University

600 West Kagy Boulevard

Bozeman, MT 59717-2730

406/994-2251 or 406/994-DINO (3466)

NATIONAL MUSEUM OF NATURAL HISTORY

(SMITHSONIAN INSTITUTION)

To see several dinosaur exhibits and special behind-the-scenes tours

10th Street and Constitution Avenue, N.W.

Washington, DC 20560-0166

202/357-2700

UNIVERSITY OF WYOMING GEOLOGY MUSEUM

To see a huge Triceratops *skull*

P.O. Box 3006,

S.H. Knight Geology Building, University of Wyoming

Laramie, WY 82071

307/766-2646

Index

About the Author

Susan H. Gray has bachelor's and master's degrees in zoology, and has taught college-level courses in biology. She first fell in love with fossil hunting while studying paleontology in college. In her 25 years as an author, she has written many articles for scientists and researchers, and many science books for children. Susan enjoys gardening, traveling, and playing the piano. She and her husband, Michael, live in Cabot, Arkansas.